TRACTOR MAC

CERTIFICATE OF REGISTRATION

This book belongs to

TRACTOR MAC
SAVES CHRISTMAS

Written and illustrated by

BILLY STEERS

FARRAR STRAUS GIROUX • NEW YORK

SNOW FELL IN BIG FAT FLAKES and blanketed Stony Meadow Farm. Tractor Mac knew the storm was coming before it started. He had seen the halo around the moon the night before, and Farmer Bill had attached wheel weights, tire chains, and the bucket loader for plowing.

Mac could see many different types of footprints in the fast-falling snow. He noticed small bird tracks and the larger tracks of Carla the chicken and the other hens.

"We're heading to the coop," clucked Carla. "It's getting too deep!" Mac used his big treads to make a tire track path for his friends.

Mac saw the tracks of the sheep in the snow.

"It's going to get much deeper," a voice said. It was Sam the ram. "They may have to cancel the town tree lighting tonight," he continued, shaking the snow from his horns.

"How could they cancel the tree lighting?" Mac asked. "What would Christmas be without it?" He remembered the carols and the hot cocoa and the gingerbread treats that were always part of the event.

"The snow is falling too fast!" said Sam. "If they can't clear the roads, people won't be able to make it to the town center."

Mac could see the snow had already reached the bottom rung of the fence.

"Moo!" called Margot the cow. "I'm worried about Sibley. Farmer Bill harnessed him up hours ago so they could fetch the town Christmas tree from the tree lot. I haven't seen them head toward town yet."

"I bet the snowman has turned them into snow sculptures," said Goat Walter. "Haven't you heard that snowmen come to life during blizzards?"

"Oh phoo, Walter," grunted Margot the cow.
"Every time there is a rumble of thunder or a hint of
snow you think something bad is lurking out there."

"There *is* something lurking out there," cried Walter, "and it's coming closer!"

Everyone strained to see through the blinding snow.

"A snowman's come to life!" shrieked Margot.
"Run for the barn!"

Snow flew in all directions as animals exploded through the drifts and ran for shelter. The shadowy, snowy figure approached Tractor Mac.

"H'lo, Mac," Farmer Bill said. Tractor Mac smiled with relief.

"Poor Sibley's tuckered out and stuck in the snow," Farmer Bill said. "I've grabbed some blankets and supplies. If we hurry, we can rescue him and save the tree-lighting ceremony."

Swoosh! Whoosh! went the blowing snow. Tractor Mac moved slowly through the thick drifts. Snow packed tight around his wheels, and he could barely feel the road beneath his tires.

They reached Sibley and the
Christmas tree, which was tied to a sled.

"I'm glad you're here, Mac," said Sibley.

"I'm tired and I can't pull this tree any farther."

Mac went straight to work.

Scoop! *Push!* **Dump!**

Scoop! *Push!* **Dump!**

He soon had Sibley out of the snowbank.

The two friends moved along till they came upon one of the town dump trucks stuck in a snowdrift.

"We were trying to clear the roads to the Christmas tree lighting," said the driver.

Scoop! *Push!* **Dump!**

Mac had them unstuck soon.

Farther along they came upon the town fire truck
wedged in a gulley. "We have lights and decorations
for the tree," said the volunteer firemen.

Scoop! *Push!* **Dump!**

Mac dug the fire truck out.

"Thanks, Mac!" said the fire truck, Number Three.
"I felt a little silly being a rescuer needing rescuing!"

Closer to town they found a school bus unable to move.

"We were taking families to the tree lighting," said the bus driver.

Farmer Bill shared his blankets with the passengers and . . .

Scoop! *Push!* **Dump!**

Tractor Mac freed the bus from the snow.

As Mac and Sibley with the big tree made their way to the center of the town green, people gathered around with shovels, brooms, and warm food. Paper bags with glowing candles helped guide them.

Everyone cheered as the beautiful evergreen was hoisted up, decorated, and lit. People sang carols and there was hot cider, hot cocoa, and cookies and cakes for everyone.

The lights reflected off the waning snowstorm, and calm filled the night.

Sibley declared, "I think we will always remember this year as the one when Tractor Mac saved Christmas!"

To my sister Kim, her husband Phil, and my wonderful nephew and niece,

Fisher and Morgan. Hoping all your days are holidays!

Farrar Straus Giroux Books for Young Readers
175 Fifth Avenue, New York 10010

Copyright © 2007 by Billy Steers
All rights reserved
Color separations by Bright Arts (H.K.) Ltd.
Printed in China by Toppan Leefung Printing Ltd.,
Dongguan City, Guangdong Province
Designed by Kristie Radwilowicz
Previous edition published by Tractor Mac, LLC
First Farrar Straus Giroux edition, 2015
1 3 5 7 9 10 8 6 4 2

mackids.com

Library of Congress Cataloging-in-Publication Data
Steers, Billy, author, illustrator.
    Tractor Mac saves Christmas / Billy Steers. — First Farrar Straus Giroux edition.
        pages cm
    Originally published in Roxbury, Connecticut, by Tractor Mac in 2007.
    Summary: When a blizzard strikes town and it looks like the tree lighting ceremony has
to be cancelled this year, Tractor Mac knows just the way to save Christmas.
    ISBN 978-0-374-30112-5 (paper over board)
    [1. Tractors—Fiction.   2. Christmas—Fiction.   3. Snow removal—Fiction.]   I. Title.

PZ7.S81536Tqt 2015
[E]—dc23

2014040408

Farrar Straus Giroux Books for Young Readers may be purchased for business or promotional
use. For information on bulk purchases please contact Macmillan Corporate and Premium
Sales Department at (800) 221-7945 x5442 or by email at specialmarkets@macmillan.com.

ABOUT THE AUTHOR

Billy Steers is an author, illustrator, and commercial pilot. In addition to the Tractor Mac series, he has worked on forty other children's books. Mr. Steers raised horses and sheep on the farm where he grew up in Roxbury, Connecticut. Married with three sons, he still lives in Roxbury. Learn more about the Tractor Mac books at www.tractormac.com.

Tractor Mac™